THE CURSE
OF THE
WINGED WIGHT

Madeline Dyer

INEJA PRESS

THE CURSE
OF THE
WINGED WIGHT

The Curse of the Winged Wight
Copyright © 2017 Madeline Dyer

Madeline Dyer asserts the moral right to be identified as the author of this work.

Second edition, July 2017
Published by Ineja Press

First appeared in *Ever in the After: 13 Fantasy Tales* in April 2017

Edited by Michelle Dunbar
Cover Art by Ravenborn, SelfPubBookCovers.com/Ravenborn

Hardcover ISBN: 978-1-912369-00-3
Paperback ISBN: 978-1-912369-01-0
eBook ISBN: 978-1-912369-02-7

The author can be contacted via email at Madeline@MadelineDyer.co.uk or through her website www.MadelineDyer.co.uk

For Rachael

PROLOGUE

Once upon a time, there was a cottage where ivy and roses grew up the walls, on trellises made of the finest willow.

The girl who lived in the cottage was beautiful. The most beautiful in all the land. Clear skin, like fresh snow, with just the right amount of blush dancing across her face. Dark eyes—big, wide, stunning. Crimson lips that one thought had to be painted on because they were so perfect. And her hair! Sleek blond locks that spilled across her shoulders, tumbling down her torso in baby ringlets.

We all know the type of girl I'm talking about. The type who is a princess—she just is. It doesn't matter that she's not the daughter of the king and queen, or that she doesn't live in a castle.

She's still the girl that every little girl wants to be.

And really, she was perfect.

So perfect, and I killed her.

ONE

"The wolves are gathering again."

My mother's voice is low, husky, as she looks out the window. I stand a few feet behind her, needle and thread still in my hands, and my eyes narrow at the cold world outside. It's been snowing for weeks, and the white blanket out there looks so soft, so inviting.

"There are four of them."

"Four?" I take a step closer, then inhale sharply as I see them.

Beautiful beings, powerful, majestic. Deadly. Every time I see them, it's the same—I'm filled with the same sense of dread, repulsion, and intrigue.

"Don't look at them," my mother says. "Shut the curtain."

I step around her wheelchair and reach the window. Outside, two of the wolves turn their heads towards me.

Their amber eyes fix me under their gaze, and I stare at them, the silver hunters. My breath catches in my throat, and I lift my hand up, touch the window. I don't know why I do it—but the action's automatic. I splay my fingers against the glass, my heart pounding. The nearest wolf moves his head slightly, and then noses the fluffy snow on the ground.

"Shut the curtain *now*, Rosanna."

My mother's voice startles me, and my hand shakes as I reach for the old fabric and—

The girl appears in front of me. On the window. No, *in* the window. In the glass itself. The girl. The same girl. It's *her*. Again. The girl with the dark hair. The girl I dreamed about last night.

My body jolts and my throat squeezes. I reach out, grab the bookcase next to me, try to steady myself.

"*Rosanna*," my mother hisses.

My heart pounds, and I look back up. But she's gone—the girl—and only eight amber eyes stare back at me.

I yank the curtain across so hard the rail shakes.

My eyes take a few moments to adjust to the new light levels, and I watch the objects form around me. The old chair my father once sat in, the box of needles and the reel of purple grosgrain ribbon on the worktable, and the spinning wheel in the far corner of the room.

And then I look at my mother. She tilts her head back slightly, her gaze on me. Even with worry etched on her face, my mother is so beautiful; with her perfect blond hair and clear blue eyes, she looks like one of the dolls I used to play with when I was little.

A tickling sensation spreads across my shoulder blades, and I pull my shawl closer around me, try and get the rough fabric grain to scratch my skin underneath.

"We need to finish the dresses," I whisper, and my hand automatically reaches for the tear-shaped scar on my neck.

"Yes," my mother says. "Light a candle. But wait a bit before you go and get the new silk."

No. Go out now.

I try to ignore the voice. But, as usual, she makes herself heard. And, as usual, I try to pretend she's not there.

"Rosanna?" My mother's voice wobbles and then her eyes widen. "Is…" Her face reddens and she looks down at her lap.

"No," I lie. "It's not."

The voice inside me laughs.

An hour later, I trudge through the village of Matakin, keeping an eye out for wolves. My feet are cold, numb. I clutch my basket to me, try to wrap my shawl tighter around me.

It doesn't take me long to get to Elyne Taylor's house. Her son answers the door. Felix seems pleased to see me. He always is. He told me before that he'd much rather marry me. But he's of class—and still has his status—so the king and queen of our kingdom choose which girl he'll marry, which bloodlines he'll strengthen.

I just wish they hadn't chosen my cousin, Carolina.

For a long time, I was sure it would be me. Even after my possessing, I thought maybe—just maybe—we could still be together. Felix is, after all, one of the few friends who didn't abandon me when the evil fairy chose me. I remember sitting on the bank with him after, and he gave me a daisy, told me that it doesn't change who I am.

But it does. You're me now and I'm you. Don't you like having me here? You're special now.

My shoulders prickle. So special that no mother would want me for their son, even if the king and queen allowed it. Not even Elyne Taylor—who's known me since birth and continues to speak to me despite the possessing—is comfortable whenever Felix and I are together. But she's never truly at ease around me now, even when I'm not with her son. During the months after my mother's spinal cord injury, when she was helping me tend to her, Elyne never spoke to me with the same warmth as she did before the evil fairy chose me. Sometimes I'm sure she thinks I'm innately bad now, because of the connection I have to the evil being inside me.

Or because, for the last seven years, my mother and I have worked for the Dark Witch. But we didn't have a choice. That's what my mother says.

"Is your mother in?" I ask Felix.

"She's just cutting out some patterns," he says, then grins. "You want to see the kittens before you get the materials?"

I set my basket down in the hallway, and brush some of the snow off my clothes. "Of course." I give him a look. "When have I ever said no?"

He grins and takes my hand, weaves me through the corridor, until we're at the back of the house, by the coal shed. Inside, he's set up a little sanctuary for the stray cats and their many kittens.

I bend down and pick up Day, my favourite. He mews, then curls up in my arms.

"Can't have the wolves eating them." Felix shakes his head. "You seen 'em in the village again?"

"There were four outside our house."

Felix nods. "Two crossed over by ours this morning. It's ridiculous. Where are they all coming from?" He takes hold of my hand. I let him. "Your mother all right?"

I nod. "She's just worried about not filling the Dark Witch's order in time. She wants twelve gowns by tomorrow. Handmade by the Mapleven line." I sigh.

"How many have you finished?"

"Seven."

He gives me a lop-sided grin. "You'll manage it. But my sisters get back later. Send a message if you're not finished, and I'll bring them down."

I press my lips together for a moment. "If the Dark Witch finds out—"

"She won't." He pulls me close, then says the words again, against my forehead. His breath is warm, and I feel myself start to relax.

I walk back to my mother's house with Felix. He won't let me walk on my own, because of the wolves. We're pass the falling tree and—

Coldness flits through my body, chased by a burning heat. The air shimmers and there's a hardness in my lungs. A moment of pain, and then it's gone. But I twist, and I look to the right—then turn, as if someone else is in control of me.

The ogress is there, ten feet away, watching me. Big and grotesque, her body sways. But she looks insubstantial. Not meaty. She's like paper.

And I know—right down to my bones—that she's not here. Not really.

They never are.

Far away, I hear Felix say my name, question why I've stopped, but his voice is too distant, and I can't turn my head back—not yet, I haven't got control yet—and all I can do is wait.

The ogress's eyes are swollen like two throbbing blood moons, and she opens her mouth, revealing thousands of pointed teeth, shining, sharp like daggers. A string of saliva hangs from one of her top teeth, and as time around me slows and stands still, I see the girl behind her. The same girl I saw in the window. The girl I'm seeing most often at the moment.

My heart pounds. My mouth dries, my tongue feels like sandpaper. I cry out but make no sound. As silent as a dream forgotten.

I can never speak when it happens.

The girl is young. Dark hair, wide blue eyes. A small tear-shaped birthmark on the left side of her face. Oh that face, how I've remembered it well.

The girl is playing in the snow, grabbing a handful, shaping it into a ball. She throws it and—

My stomach roils as the ogress grabs her. An ear-shattering squeal that only I can hear, a squeal that turns into a nail and punctures my soul and keeps on digging.

I try to look away again, but can't.

Punishment.

The word flashes through me.

And it all happens in less than a second. All of it—the vision, the murder; a blink of an eye and it's gone—yet it's inside me, etched onto my brain, and it stretches out, distorts time.

"Rosanna?" Felix looks at me.

I look at him. I've stopped—but I know I've only stopped for a second.

I've always had the visions of the dead girls, the murders—they started long before the evil fairy got me; before the Dark Witch said she'd help. The visions started as nightmares, and my parents took me to a healer when I was little. The man said I had an overactive imagination. But then I started seeing the girls when I was awake too, and it worried my mother immensely. The visits to the healers became more frequent, and even after the possessing and my mother's injury, she continued paying the ones who'd still see me, begging them to get rid of my visions. Neither of us wanted to make another deal with the Dark Witch, who, upon learning of my visions, had offered to look into them once our first deal's fulfilled.

"Are you okay?" Felix's voice makes me jump, and I turn—free now—and look at him. There is a tenderness in his eyes that nearly melts the ice in my heart.

I nod, breathe deeply, and try to shake it all off. "Let's just get back."

But that's been two visions. And I can't help wondering what that can mean. Two visions during the daytime alone...and the day's not over yet.

The dead girls won't leave me alone.

TWO

The Dark Witch fixes me under one beady eye. The other inspects the dresses. All twelve of them.

I shift my weight from foot-to-foot and try to keep my breathing steady. We're in the large hallway of her castle, and the red carpet smells strange, musty. The walls around us are covered in vibrant tapestries, and, above, the chandelier sways slightly. But there's no wind in here, no movement at all. Yet the tiny bulbs with their long, trailing crystal chains sway back and forth.

I swallow hard and look at the Dark Witch. Her left eye is still on me, the other on the dresses spread across her side-table.

Every time I enter the castle, I think of the first day I saw her. It was three months after the possessing and my mother's accident when the Dark Witch trekked into

Matakin and showed up at our door. She said she'd heard of the recent events and had travelled the lands for months, until she came upon the Snow Kingdom and found me. She was fascinated by me and wanted to touch my hand, but I was too scared. I'd only just turned ten years old.

My mother did most of the talking that day, even though she was weak and had only just come home. I remember how scared I was, how the moment I'd opened the door and let the Dark Witch in, a bad feeling had settled into the pit of my stomach, and I'd scurried to the side of the room. My mother was sitting in her chair in the middle of the living room and the Dark Witch was leering over her, looking like a predator, ready to swipe and kill. But my mother was so calm. They talked as I stood by the staircase, shaking and trembling as I looked towards the open front door, waiting for Elyne to walk up the path because it was time for my mother's toilet trip.

But Elyne didn't come, and the Dark Witch whispered about connections and how long it had been. She wanted to know about *me* and whether the evil fairy had spoken into my mind. My mother said no, but I knew that she knew the truth. We've always been close like that.

"But can you save her?" my mother asked. "Please, I'll do anything! Just get rid of the wicked entity!"

Ha! Wicked, indeed. I haven't even controlled your body, made you do anything! I'm just here.

And the Dark Witch nodded. "Work for me for twenty years—make my dresses—both of you, and I will give you food and clothes, and when the time comes, I will help Rosanna Mapleven find the fairy who possesses her. Help rid your daughter of her." Her voice was like a raspy snake as she said my name.

But it wasn't my name. Not then. I was Rosanna Hawthorne then, but the Dark Witch told us to cut my father out, and that I must take my mother's maiden name as my own. From then on, I've been Rosanna Mapleven. And part of me was glad to cut my father off when he'd disowned me because I was tainted, and not bothered to help his own wife after her back had been broken.

I remember the way the Dark Witch smiled as she said goodbye, that first time, showing us her bronze-coated teeth, and I remember the dark feeling that had settled in the pit of my stomach. It's a feeling I could never shake off, and a few weeks later, when we heard the Dark Witch had moved into the abandoned castle outside the village, I'd got sick for months. My illness had made it hard to make the dresses on time—especially given my mother was still struggling with the use of her arms and hands—but somehow, we'd managed it.

"Exquisite." The Dark Witch runs her fingers over the fine embroidery on the bodices. "Really exquisite." Then she grabs my hand before I have a chance to move. "Have eight more done for tomorrow tonight, with jewel necklines and scallops. I want some edgy shapes."

"Eight?" I can't help myself, and I wince as the word flies out.

"*Ten*." Her eyes flash. "Twelve! Fourteen! And vipers! I want vipers—vipers and frogs embroidered on the sashes—each dress must have a sash."

I bow and retreat as quickly as I can. As I walk away from the Dark Witch's castle, I hear the voice. The night crawls with her words.

Come and join me. Find me.

I jump and push the words way, concentrate on my breathing and the different sensations in my body. After a while, my shoulder blades start to itch again. I concentrate on that itching and not the evil fairy's command. Her new instruction. *Join me.*

The road to Matakin is lonely, lined by old oak trees on either side. I reach the brow of the hill, look down and—

I freeze. The hairs on the back of my neck rise.

A wolf. A big one. A hundred feet away.

I move slowly, carefully, step behind a tree and watch, hold my breath. Its eyes seem to glow—as red as the sun—and I see a dusting of blood around its muzzle.

It pads towards the village and—

I see the two children coming before it does.

And I try to warn them—I step out from my tree, wave my arms as fast as I can. But they're caught up in a game, laughing and shrieking. Their cries of excitement are delivered in the wind to me. And they're small, the children are so small.

The wolf sees them. It stops, and then it stands up straighter. It cranes its head forward.

Then it runs towards them.

I cry out—but I know there's nothing I can do now. Nothing at all. Nothing but watch as the wolf grabs the first child, its jaws clamping around his throat. The wolf shakes the boy. I hear a squeak, and then the child is limp.

The other little boy stands frozen to the spot. The wolf looks up at him.

I look away, and I wait. Somehow, I know that the wolf will leave without seeing me, without hurting me.

And it does, dragging one of the dead children with it.

And when it's gone, I sprint.

By the time I get home, I am shaking, and I can't rid

my head of the images or sounds. The blood. The amber eyes, burning with ferocity and adrenaline and the kills. The screams. The cries. It all followed me, chased me as I ran through the woods, down to the village, my feet skidding in the snow. Even the slam of the front door wasn't enough to break the echo of the screams.

"It's getting worse." My mother sits by the worktable with Elyne and Felix, and her voice wobbles. But then she takes one look at me, and she knows what I have seen. My mother's always been like that. We're connected. Of the same soul, she often says.

Felix rises and wraps me in his arms. I lean into him, shaking.

"Careful," Elyne says. "You know you cannot have Rosanna Mapleven."

I feel Felix's body tense as he holds me. He ignores his mother.

"Something needs to be done about the wolves," is all he says.

The next morning, just as I'm taking the loaf of bread out the oven, and wondering whether I've got time to eat the leftover chicken from last night, my cousin and her parents arrive. Carolina Mapleven—a dazzling beauty, wrapped in a red silk dress—lights up our hut with her glowing presence, but her parents drag the light levels back down with their frowns. The three of them are our only relatives who still visit us. My mother says it is only because they want to emphasise their wealth, show off what they've got, what we haven't. And because Aunt Keres never misses an opportunity to boast about her job at the Royal Castle.

Carolina looks at the bread with the eye of an eagle. She smells the bread, and her nostrils flare into wide circles that mirror the gemstones and preserved rose heads wrapped in her hair—beautifully styled golden hair that's the exact same shade as my mother's. Then she smiles and grabs a knife. "It smells good, Rosanna. Excellent. When are we cutting it?"

"You can't cut bread until prayers have been said," her mother says. Keres Mapleven has the voice of an angel, but the heart of the devil. That's what my father always said, back in the days when he still lived with us.

"Absolutely—oh Lord, you aren't using that knife, are you?" Carolina's father, Nabal—my mother's brother— glares at me. "Look at the rust on that! Here, Carolina, go out to our carriage and fetch some decent cutlery. We can't use that knife—put it down at once!"

My mother and I exchange looks as Carolina leaves.

My uncle begins to inspect the window sills—*"My, what dust there is! You should definitely get a cleaner!"*—and my aunt inspects me. I shudder. I checked myself in the small mirror this morning and washed all the grime off my face.

"You're getting thin," Aunt Keres says and blinks her dark eyes at me rapidly. They're the same shade as my eyes. "Just skin and bone! You need more meat on you, girl." She turns quickly to my mother, and the strong smell of stale, slimy water wafts towards me. "Louisa, do you even feed her?"

"With more tenderness than your daughter will ever know," my mother replies tartly. She straightens her skirt, brushes non-existent dirt from it, and then folds her hands on her lap.

We're both wearing our finest gowns, but they're nothing compared to what we make for the Dark Witch day in, day out. More than once, I've wondered why the Dark Witch needs so many dresses, especially when she always wears the same black robe.

"At the Royal Castle, food is in abundance," my aunt says. "And we can each have as much as we want. Only last week, I was discussing plans with Her Royal Highness for the new orchards and farming pens. It really is magnificent there—oh, my mouth's watering just thinking about the turkey I tasted only last week! It was almost as good as the poultry that the monarch of the Silver Land brought with him on his last visit to our Royal Castle—and that was spectacular."

And with that, my aunt descends into every little detail about how wonderful her life is. I try to look interested, and I can't help but notice the tension in my mother's fists as she clenches her hands together tightly in her lap.

After a while, Carolina nudges me. "It must be nice having your mother live with you all the time," she says in a low voice. "My mother's only here for the day, and then she's got to go back to the Royal Castle. Another eight weeks before her next day off. She always promises I can visit her there, during an evening when there's less work for her to do, but it never happens." Carolina's face darkens. "She just won't take me there."

I squeeze her hand.

For the next hour or so, I watch my aunt and uncle evaluate our house. Prayers to the High Ones are said, the bread is cut with a fine silver knife, and we eat. The whole time I think about the dressmaking I could be doing instead.

Then the topic of conversation moves onto Felix. Just as I knew it would.

"We're thinking of a summer wedding. Six months' time," Aunt Keres begins. "I've got the dress that all the Larne, Noble, and Mapleven brides have worn—it's important to keep it in the right bloodline. And Carolina will look delightful in the gown, just like the beautiful princess who hides inside her—but you two would have to dress up a little. You look like servants in those clothes."

My uncle's eyes widen. He gestures at us, then looks at his wife. "Do you think…think it is wise? We don't want to upset the king and queen, and they *will* be at the ceremony."

Upset them. With me. I resist a snort.

Yessssss. I'm part of you. Now, listen to—

I block her voice out.

"But, Mother!" Carolina cries. "Of course Rosanna and Aunt Louisa *have* to come—it is a family occasion." Carolina gives me a quick smile. "And it was awfully unfair that they lost their status like that. It wasn't their fault! Rosanna was just in the wrong place at the wrong time. That evil fairy could've got *anyone*."

Looking at my cousin, I wonder whether we ever could've been friends.

"The invites can be sorted at a later date," Uncle Nabal says.

My mother disguises a snort as a cough. "How convenient."

"Well, we must be going." Aunt Keres stands up. She holds a hand against her stomach for a moment, and her face looks strangely green. "I'm due back at the Royal Castle shortly, and it is such a long journey. I must leave ample time for it."

"How lovely seeing you two again," my uncle says. But he doesn't look at me as he says the words, only my mother.

When they've gone, it's as if the air is free again, not chained up. I breathe deeply, feeling exhausted, like I've been running the length of the village all morning.

My mother wheels herself to the worktable and opens the cupboard under it.

"We must be quick now," she says, pulling out sheaves of patterns and a roll of bead elastic. "Four bodices, jewelled and moon-soaked, still need to be made. Can you get the new amethysts? And the appliqué scissors must be upstairs too."

I head up to my room. The majority of the materials were put up here this morning in an attempt to tidy up before the visit.

I pull out the bag of amethysts, and a sheet of paper

falls to the floor. I pick it up. A note.

It's written in big black letters, sprawled across newsprint. My eyes focus on the printed paragraphs, and I pick out the words *shame*, *death*, and *time* in the background.

And then I read the sprawled words, and something happens to my body. I feel strange, lighter, and pain shoots down my spine. I lift my head up, look out the window and—

A girl watches me, her face pressed to the glass. She breathes out and the window fogs. Her mouth opens. She mouths my name—*Rosanna*—and then the evil fairy joins in.

Rosanna! Rosanna! Rosanna!

My chest squeezes.

I look back down at the paper.

YOUR SEVENTEENTH BIRTHDAY IS COMING. BLOOD WILL SPILL, AND A GIRL WILL FALL.

THREE

Just before last light, the Taylors come over and help my mother and I finish the dresses. We've only got the top stitching to do and the final embellishments. With six of us, it takes no time at all, and then Felix escorts me to the Dark Witch's castle with the goods. He pulls the trailer, and it bobs along behind us.

Everywhere I look, I see the words from the paper. The warning.

And I hear the words too; they're whispered on the wind, enclosed in the flurries of snow. They're all around me.

Your seventeenth birthday is coming. Blood will spill, and a girl will fall.

My breath catches in my throat, makes a squeaky noise. My hand goes to my pocket where the note is, but I know the paper will be blank now. The message disappeared within seconds of me reading it.

Gone, forever forgotten except to my mind.

Or maybe I imagined it. Because I've never seen words like that before. The visions, they're always of the girls or an ogress, or both.

Never a message written down.

I touch my head slowly, cautiously. Am I going mad? Was I already mad?

Everyone is scared of madness, that's one thing I learned at school, back when I used to go. Mr Penny went mad. Tara said the wolves came for him in the night, that they drunk his blood because madness is sweeter than sanity.

And it's always the *seventeenth* birthday that was important in the stories I read as a child. The entrance into adulthood. The doorway to the future. The time when madness can really grow and flourish in a person.

"Almost there," Felix says.

The wind picks up, and the air gets bitterer. A crisp bite to it. I pull my shawl around me tighter as I look up at the castle. The old building towers over us. Only two high turrets made from burnt orange stone still reach into the sky, proud and sombre. All that's left of the ancient columns on the western side are the broken stones scattered down the hillside. The Dark Witch only uses the rooms on the eastern side, but, a couple of years ago, she told me she was thinking of restoring the rest of her home, now that she's settled.

The Dark Witch's only footman greets us at the small iron gate in front of the huge oak doors. His smile is wary. It always is when he sees me. But the Dark Witch insists that *I* am to bring each batch of dresses.

"The Dark Witch has gone away," the footman says, his voice nervous. He looks me up and down, then Felix.

"Great," Felix says. "These are the clothes she ordered from the Maplevens." He glances at me briefly.

I just nod and rub my hands together. My fingers are pink with the cold, and I notice how red Felix's nose has gone.

Come, join me, Rosanna. Come and find me now, find me—

I stiffen. The same command as yesterday. I stare at the trees, the snow-covered ground, the heavy sky.

"What is it?" Felix's voice is low, and he touches my arm, makes me jump.

I turn back. "Nothing."

Blood must spill. A girl must fall.

Rossssssanna.

Come and find me, give yourself to me, and I will

show you how…

We're of the same soul, I know what you must do. Find me!

I hear her words, her instructions, the whole way back to the village. They follow me. And she keeps whispering. And I keep looking, turning—expecting to see something—and Felix keeps watching me dubiously, his bottom lip sticking out slightly.

"Are you sure you're okay?" Felix's words press against my forehead as he holds me outside my house.

I nod, breathe in his scent. The slight muskiness of his old coat. Part of me still doesn't know why he likes me, why he's still here.

I was expelled from the school, blamed for any worse-than-usual weather that occurred, and berated for the high food prices at the market.

People became scared of me, nervous, wary. I'm *tainted*. I'm bad.

But not Felix, he stayed, insisted it didn't mean I was any different. Sometimes I wonder if he's wrong.

"You seem a bit jumpy." Felix pauses. "I'm sure the Dark Witch will like the dresses. Don't worry, Rose."

The Dark Witch. Something about those words makes me shudder, makes my spine feel as if icy water is being dripped down it.

Yessssss, the evil fairy says.

"I'm just tired."

"Get an early night then. I'll see you tomorrow."

"Tomorrow?"

He smiles as he pulls away from me. "It's your day off, and I've got a surprise for you." The light catches his dark hair, makes the bronze flecks in it shine. "Be ready bright and early."

"But, my mother—"

"I've cleared it with her. Just get plenty of rest. You'll need your energy tomorrow."

I can't help but smile as I watch him leave. Can't help the way my fingers feel warm and fuzzy. Can't help how I suddenly entertain the idea of running away with him, taking him somewhere far, far away where there are no rules to keep us apart, and no Carolina.

.

FOUR

I get up with the early sun the following morning and feel strangely light, energised, despite my troubled sleep. Too many dreams. Fragments of conversations, images that didn't make sense. But, at the same time, there was a sense of familiarity, of knowing—and it's that sense that haunts me, as if it's got tiny fingers and each finger is grabbing hold of me and insisting that I remember, that I listen, that I know. Holding on tightly, never to let go.

I hear my mother in the room below; the slight squeak of her chair, and a small thud as she drops something. A moment later, scratchy sounds follow, and I frown. Then there's another voice. A voice I know well.

When I get downstairs, I see Felix sitting by our Rayburn, a recipe book in his hands. My mother's at the table, squashing several small packages into a basket.

Felix smiles widely, then stands, takes me in his arms.

"What?" I start to say, but he puts a finger to my lips. And I'm so close to him. I can feel his heart beating—feel it as if it's part of me. As if we're the same person, the same heart.

And I'm so aware of my mother watching.

I step back.

"Are you ready?" Felix asks.

I look from side to side. The kitchen looks cleaner, and the broom isn't in the right place. Felix's been sweeping the floor for my mother?

"I haven't eaten breakfast yet," I say, frowning.

"We'll eat when we get there," he says. "Your mother's packed us a feast."

I turn quizzically to my mother.

She smiles. "Go."

The light is beautiful. We're high up on the mountain, and far, far below, I can see Matakin lazily spread out like a toy village. I narrow my eyes, feel the wind rush against my face, manage to pick out the area where my mother's hut is. The trees shield it from sight though.

Four hours it took us to walk here, but it was worth it. And eating the picnic was magical up here. I feel like I'm on top of the world. I look down at the other part of the village, to the cottage where Carolina and her father live. Far to the left, on the snow-covered hills, a pack of wolves roam. I narrow my eyes, count them. Twelve.

"I spoke to old Foggy Lily a few days ago," Felix says.

"Foggy Lily?" I raise my eyebrows at the mention of the batty woman who thinks she can see the future.

"Yeah. We spoke about the wolves." A slight smile graces his lips.

"What did she say?"

"That soon a guardian angel with a bow and arrow will protect the villagers and the wolves will move away."

"A guardian angel?" My eyebrows rise even higher, and I try not to laugh.

"Oh, there's more," Felix says. "Listen to this: apparently, I'll *know* the angel. I'll recognise her. I won't like her then, when I see her—though Foggy Lily was really vague, you know what she's like—but she said there was still a chance for the angel and me, that our future could still be written. Ha, imagine that."

I snort. "Well, at least that's one of her nicer stories. She told my mother that she'd lose her only daughter. I guess she's right…with me being possessed and all that."

And my seventeenth birthday is looming.

Blood will spill, and a girl will fall.

My death? When I'm seventeen?

I swallow hard, don't know why I think of the words, not when they don't mean anything. And that note—I don't even know if it happened, if I trust myself, trust my memory.

"They're just stories," Felix says. "Don't take any notice. Just enjoy being up here."

I lean back against the mossy rocks; we brushed snow from them earlier, though, strangely, there wasn't as much up here as down in Matakin. I try to relax. After a moment, I look across at Felix.

He's so close, the side of his body only inches from mine. I look into his eyes—those clear, blue eyes. There are whole worlds in those eyes, sparkling life that grabs me, that pulls me in deeper and deeper until I'm drowning, until—

His lips brush against mine.

My eyes close, and then I'm sinking, sinking in the world—in his world—as everything rushes by.

When I open them again, he's watching me, an amused look on his face. He smiles. "I've got a plan."

"A plan?"

He nods. "And I want to tell you my plan, while it's just the two of us. While nothing else matters."

"Okay… What is it?"

"It's Carolina's birthday soon."

My shoulders tighten and the skin across my upper back prickles. "I know." It's also *my* birthday that day too. "You'll get engaged then. Officially."

He shakes his head. "We won't if she's…not…not available."

My eyes widen. "What?"

"It would solve all the problems," he says, "if she wasn't…about. And *we* could be together then."

I feel the evil fairy stir within me.

"And," he continues. "It would be so easy. My mother knows a healer—invites her around all the time, and she often brings her bag because she's treating patients beforehand, you know. And a lot of those concoctions, if you take too much then it does more harm than good."

I stare at him, feel my stomach harden. "You want to *poison* my cousin?" My words come out a lot louder than expected, and I look around as if expecting someone else to have overheard. But there's no one here.

Just us two and—

I blink and see a girl's face. A fraction, and it's gone. I stiffen.

"No—no, I didn't say that," Felix says. "I *want* to be with you."

"You did say that." I frown, swallow hard. I blink again—several times—but I don't see her face again. I turn to Felix. "That's exactly what you said—what you suggested, anyway."

"I just want to be with you." He runs his hands through his dark hair. "There's got to be a way—and this way…" He leans forwards suddenly. "Look, Rose, you've got a dark fairy in you. You could ask her to do it, we don't even have to do it ourselves."

I stare at him. "*Murder*? You're actually suggesting murder?"

Blood must spill. A girl must fall. Curses must repeat, even if they twist and evolve.

My blood feels icy as it pumps through me. *Those* words. Her—my evil fairy? *She* put them there? I frown, feel my heartbeat get heavier.

"It doesn't have to be murder—that wasn't what I meant…just something." Felix throws his hands up in the air. "I don't know. My sister pricked her finger on the distaff when she was spinning, and it became infected. My mum had to take her over to an advanced healer, and they were away for ages. There must be something like that that could happen to Carolina. Just *something* to get her out of the way for a bit. Your birthday's the same as Carolina's, and that's when you both become adults. If she's well and healthy, then the engagement will be officially announced. But if she's not, then *we* could run away and get married."

"If she's not well enough on the day, they'll just postpone the announcement," I point out. "You're already intended for her. The official announcement doesn't actually make it real. It's still going to happen."

"But *without* the official announcement when we're both of age, the wedding can't go ahead. Not until the engagement *is* announced. But, if I'm already married—to you—then I can't marry her when she's better."

"No priest would go against the king and queen's wishes and marry us." I shake my head. "The king and queen don't want me marrying anyone."

He presses his lips together for a long moment. "A priest would for the right price. If I found one, could you ask your dark fairy for help with incapacitating Carolina? You could make it look like an accident or something."

"*No*." I shake my head. "Absolutely not. She's still my cousin."

"But I don't want to be with her." Felix's eyes flash. **Blood *will* spill.**

"No!" I yell, feel heat rush to my hands and my face. Felix jumps.

I breathe deeply. "Carolina is my cousin. I don't want to hurt her."

Yessssss, you do. You're jealous of her, and you want Felix for yourself. I can tell. And it would be so easy to do...

Felix's pupils get a tiny bit bigger. "And I guess that's why I love you," he says. "I'm sorry. I'm just..." He breathes deeply.

Then he kisses me again, but the moment's gone.

FIVE

It happened when I was nine years old.

I was at the barn where the village children have their lessons, and the sky turned red. Everyone knew what that meant, and the teachers were panicking but pretending they weren't. Children were crying. Passing parents were rushing in, trying to find their babies.

I don't know why, but I walked out into the field. When healers hear that, they think it means I'd already been chosen by the evil fairy, that she was compelling me to go there, to make it easier for her to finish her work.

But Felix says I wanted to see the flowers. There were bluebells on the bank at the far side, and he says he'd just told me about them—about how beautiful the display was. I've always loved bluebells. Even more than daisies and roses. And it's rare that the snow stops for long enough in this kingdom for any spring flowers to bloom.

So I was outside. Standing amongst the knee-high grass, when a fork of lightning crashed down from the red sky.

It split the ground—a crack between worlds, infused with magic.

And I heard her voice.

Come and help me. Please, help me. Please, baby.

She sounded like my mother. Maybe that was why I followed her voice. Why I walked up to the burning hole in the ground, why I didn't panic when I saw her: a woman, with wings made of black feathers that looked so beautiful, so enticing.

An apparition projected from afar with fey magic. That was what the people called it later.

But to me she didn't look like an apparition. She didn't waver about, or flicker, or seem insubstantial—not like how the ogress often looks in my visions.

She just seemed like a sad woman. A sad woman who'd asked me to help her, who'd spoken with so much kindness and tenderness. How was I supposed to know that it was a trick?

That she'd grab me.

That she'd live inside me, *possess* me, try and talk to

me.

I was just nine years old.

I didn't know.

I just wanted to help.

And in the midst of it, my mother. Somehow, she appeared in it all. She was just there—she said later that she felt that something was wrong—and her hands were on my arm, trying to drag me away.

I remember her screaming—screams that chilled me, that shook me, that made me realise what was happening.

I remember running—or trying to run, because my legs were so heavy. And then a flash of blue light.

My feet turning on the ground.

My mother's screams, like a vixen's.

My mother's body, limp, several feet away.

And she, the evil fairy, disappeared.

But her mark was on me, in me, all over me.

I was hers.

That night, at home, my father took one look at me— one look at the scar on my neck, the evil fairy's mark—then he turned and left.

He didn't ask which healer my mother was with or how badly her back was broken. He didn't ask whether she'd be able to walk again. For weeks I told myself that maybe he didn't know what my mother had done, that she'd tried to stop the evil fairy and had failed—that he didn't *know* she was injured. But deep down, I knew that he only saw me now for what I'd become: the tainted girl. And what I would cause.

Maybe he thought that if he left, the king and queen might not take his status away as well.

But either way, he left.

And neither my mother nor I have seen him since.

"Any success lately?"

Agatha Tapleman, an old woman who says she used to be the best healer in the kingdom, points at me as she speaks, and I stare at the warts on her face. They're like little mountains, and somehow there are even more of them protruding from her dried-apricot skin than last month.

I shake my head. "No."

"Any changes?"

I've had the visions more frequently, but I don't tell her that. I've always seen the girls—that's nothing to do with the evil fairy. Instead, I tell the old woman that the evil fairy's been speaking to me a lot more. That she told me to find her and join her, something she's never said before.

"Interesting, dear." The old woman frowns.

We're in her hut, on the other side of Matakin. Agatha Tapleman is one of the few people who'll even see me. And she believes she might still be able to get rid of my visions *and* the evil fairy.

But she's not magic—that's what my mother had pointed out. Only magic can undo magic. But waiting twenty years for the Dark Witch to save me is too long.

It's been years already, and I'm desperate. My mother's desperate.

"Of course," Agatha Tapleman says. "You may be hearing the evil fairy's instructions more, given it is closer to your seventeenth birthday." She looks down at her notes. "Days away, in fact."

"My seventeenth birthday?" I press my lips together slowly, feel the blood drain from my face. My heart speeds up. "What? Why?"

"I was doing some research in the archives at the Royal Castle," Agatha Tapleman says. "And I found an old, old book. Mr Scuttle showed it to me. All about ancient lore and dealings with wicked beings. In it, a pastor describes the possessing of his young daughter and how the evil being only got control of her—complete control—upon her seventeenth birthday."

Your seventeenth birthday is coming. Blood will spill,

and a girl will fall.

Because the evil fairy will take control of me then?

Blood will spill…

She'll get me to kill and—oh, God. Didn't she…when Felix was talking about Carolina, about making her sleep, about hurting her…didn't the evil fairy agree with him…say it would be easy and—

I clap a hand to my mouth, feeling sick.

Carolina—no!

"Perhaps another visit to the archives is required," Agatha Tapleman says. "But there are thousands of records to go through. We'll need an army."

I look down at my lap, then back up. "My aunt works there. Well, at the Royal Castle."

Agatha Tapleman frowns. "What's her name?"

"Keres Mapleven."

"I haven't heard of her. But perhaps we could ask her to help us in our search, save some time."

"Perhaps," I mutter.

As if.

Agatha Tapleman suddenly stands up. "For the time being, stop taking the peppermint concoction—in case that's making the wight stronger, making her speak to you more." She shuffles her notes. "Instead, take three drops of dew each morning and a rose petal. The night before, soak the petal in purified water with a sprig of rosemary and a pinch of garlic. Three drops of the dew directly to the tongue, and chew the petal. Let me know in three days' time if there's any difference. If not, we'll have to try something new. Though there's not much time until your birthday arrives."

My mother glances up when I arrive home.

"Well?"

"More potions," I mutter.

My mother sets her needle and thread on the table, amongst the tracing paper and twill tape, then tuts under her breath. "The Dark Witch is our only option."

"It's no option at all if the evil fairy gets full control of me on my birthday," I cry and look at my mother.

She sighs. "That is just lore—"

"You knew about it? That it's a possibility?"

"There's no proof for that, Rosanna, and you know it. The Dark Witch must know it's a fable too. She wouldn't have offered us this deal if the wicked being consumes you, takes control of you, before then. Now, did you see any more wolves out there?"

I shake my head.

"Come here."

My mother takes my hand when I reach her. "Try not to worry. That evil being isn't going to get you. You're going to enjoy your birthday like any other girl would. We'll have a party, here."

I frown. "A party? Mum, I haven't exactly got many friends."

"You've got Felix."

I flinch. "You know where he's going to be on my birthday."

And just the thought sends dark feelings deep into my core.

"He won't be at your cousin's all day—"

"He will if Uncle Nabal has any say in it. He knows about me and Felix, and he'll do anything to make sure that he's with Carolina for the whole of her birthday." I sigh. "Maybe it's best though, if I am going to turn into an evil person."

Blood will spill, and a girl will fall, Rosanna.

I shudder. I don't know why I think of the words then—or why I imagine my mother saying them.

SIX

I drag the next trailer full of dresses towards the Dark Witch's castle and think about what might be in the next hamper of food the Dark Witch sends us. The delivery usually comes once a month, and lately she's been putting more meat into it. I never used to like meat that much, but recently, I've found myself craving it. A joint of lamb with Sauce Robert. A slice of gammon with roast potatoes. A nice roast chicken with gravy.

Come, join me.

I try to ignore the voice, try to think about the food, but it's louder this time.

I walk through the snowy lands. My body feels strangely warm. The cold fingers of the icy wind barely touch me.

Come, join me.

My feet move faster, I move faster, catch a glimpse of myself in a frozen puddle. My eyes are burning—burning like fire. A furious fire.

I blink, startled, and step back.

You can't hide who you really are. And you need me as much as I need you. Come now. Come on, Rosanna. I was always going to get you. It's in our blood.

I try to ignore her voice.

But you won't be able to ignore her for much longer— not once you're seventeen and she controls you. That thought doesn't make me feel any better, even though I know there's no certainty that it will happen.

The Dark Witch is waiting for me when I get to her castle. One glance, and she knows what Felix was planning—I can tell by the way her lips twitch and lift at the corners, how her body shakes with excitement. I just know—and the realisation sits strangely in me. I shouldn't know. But I do.

Yessssss.

"This way," the Dark Witch says. "This way, my girl."

I shudder, and part of me is confused by the tenderness she shows to me sometimes. Most people are scared of me, because of the mark. But not the Dark Witch.

Daughter, the evil fairy whispers.

My skin crawls.

I breathe deeply, and I follow the Dark Witch.

We go to a room at the back of her castle, one I've never been to before. She searches deep inside a cupboard. I look out the window.

It's still snowing. Always snowing.

In the distance, a wolf howls.

I look around the room, and for the first time, I realise how lonely this castle is. How lonely the Dark Witch must be, living here on her own. Sure, she has her footman for company, on the few days he works for her, but I've never seen the two speak. He's terrified of her.

And then, for some reason, I think of Carolina—how lonely she is without her mother's love.

Still, she has her father.

The Dark Witch has no one.

"Here is it, daughter." The Dark Witch's voice startles me, and I turn back, get the feeling I've been standing here for a long, long time.

She holds out a drawing to me.

I take it. The drawing is old, very old. Done in charcoal. It's a girl—one of the girls I've seen for the longest, one of the ones I've watched get killed by the ogress, many, many times. I look at her face, and now I can't help but see it, concentrate on it—the way her hair curls slightly on one side of her head more than the other, how her eyes are grey, yet there's warmth there too. And the birthmark on her chin.

I reach up. Touch my own. It's on my neck, in a different place, but I realise it's the same. Tear-shaped. How didn't I notice before?

And we—the girl and me…we do look similar.

I stare at the photo. "Who is she?"

"You should already know the answer to that," the Dark Witch croaks. "Put the pieces together. Save my daughter."

And then she touches my face. Her hands are cold, so cold. She stares into my eyes, and I feel something move inside me.

"The cycle must stop, my precious. The circle must end."

SEVEN

When I close my eyes, I see the girl again. The one from the visions, the one from the Dark Witch's drawing.

And I see her, properly see her.

And she *is* me.

The same dark hair. The same small nose. The same high cheekbones.

Yet she has the mark on her chin, not her neck… She's me, and yet she's not.

She's standing in the woods, a cloak wrapped around her shoulders. A big red cloak.

And I'm standing behind her. I call out to her, but my words are soundless, and she doesn't turn. I walk up to her, circle her, but she doesn't react.

She just stares ahead.

A few minutes later, a boy rides up on his horse. He dismounts, kisses the girl, and—

"No!" I scream as the ogress appears, several feet away, mainly hidden by the trees.

I catch a glimpse of the knife in the boy's belt, a moment before the ogress grabs it and plunges it through the girl's back.

Her eyes widen, and she makes a choking sound, and—

There's no birthmark now. Her face is clear and—

It was there but...

It's her, but…

But *not*.

Changing. She's changing.

Her scream is different.

Different.

Different.

Different.

A different girl?

Then the boy looks at me. *Really* looks at me.

"You're next," he says, and the ogress moves in, picks up the girl's body, and sinks her teeth into flesh. The boy just stares at me. "You will die next."

I wake, gasping for breath, panting hard, covered in sweat. I look up at the window and—

Two girls are there. Two girls whom I've seen before—years ago…when I was eleven. I saw them regularly then, for nearly a year. Long brown hair, small dainty noses, wide eyes.

One girl breathes on the window.

The other lifts her finger, writes on the fogged glass.

Watch out, Rosanna.

My heart pounds.

The girls disappear.

Watch out. Watch out. Watch out, the evil fairy whispers. Then she laughs.

I laugh, and the sound bursts from me, shocks me. I freeze, heart racing faster and faster. Why did I laugh? Why?

I look back at the window. The words are still there, still on the glass.

It's real.

In one quick motion, I jump up, race across the floor, to the stairs. In seconds, I'm down there, sprinting across the front room. Need to find them, have to find them. That wasn't a dream—the girl in the woods with the boy and the ogress—it can't have been.

It was…something more.

My heart pounds as I unlock the front door, as I step into the cold night. Snow buffets my body, and cold, invisible hands try to push me back in.

"Hello?" I call out. My voice sounds tinny, lost.

The darkness seems to get darker, but the snow gets lighter, brighter, as if it's emitting its own light.

I run across the snow, my steps light. As if I'm not stepping down at all, as if I weigh nothing. And my feet— my bare feet—they don't feel the snow, or the cold.

"Where are you?" I look back and forth, try to see the girls.

But I can't find them.

There are no footprints out here. Not even…not even mine. I look back the way I came, and my eyes widen. That's…that's not right…there should be…should be something, should be—

I turn and freeze as I see my heavy shadow. See it in the snow, where it shouldn't be because there shouldn't be enough light to make a shadow but—

In my shadow, two shapes protrude from my back. Rough triangles.

I look over my shoulder, see nothing. I look at my feet. My bare feet, in the snow. Lift one up, see the indentation below. A footprint. But there are none around me.

I frown, and then I'm shaking with the cold. I walk back towards my front door. I left it open.

You shouldn't leave doors open. Anyone could walk in.

Her voice makes me jump, and I look around, but the sky's darkening, and the snow's a murky fortress building around me. My breathing slows a little as I close the door, listen carefully. My mother's room is just on the left, but there are no sounds of her stirring. I listen for a few more minutes, then head back upstairs.

The first thing I look at is my window. I walk right up to it, to the place where the words were written. But they're not there now. I tilt my head to the left side, then the right, peering closer at the glass, trying to see something, anything left behind.

But there's nothing.

I turn and look at my bookcase. The Dark Witch's drawing of the girl stares back at me.

The cycle must stop.

I rub my eyes, then reach for my duvet, pull it back and—

A scream builds in my throat as I see the knife. The knife on my pillow. The knife that wasn't there before. The knife covered in blood.

The knife used to murder the girl in my dream.

It's the same one.

And blood will spill again. We shall spill blood again.

EIGHT

I race to my mother's room, heart pounding, throw the door open.

My mother jolts awake. "What is it, Rosanna?"

And then she sees the knife in my hand, because her eyes widen, and I don't know why I'm holding it, why I'm gripping it so tightly, pointing the blade at her, with only her wheelchair between us.

"Oh, Lord," she whispers, her face paling. "It's happening."

I freeze. Stare at the knife in my hand. And it feels good, like it's supposed to be there. My fingers have curled around it, a cage for the weapon.

Yessssss.

I drop the knife.

It clanks on the floor, and specs of blood fly from it.

"What have you done?" My mother's voice twists into me, stronger now. "Rosanna, what have you done?"

They all said it. All the teachers at school said I was bad, that the evil fairy would make me do stuff. It didn't matter that she'd not taken control of my body as a true possessing would—I was still *possessed*, whether she chose to use my body or not. She was still there, in me. I was part of her, she was part of me, and we'd do bad stuff.

But I don't believe it. Because I know I haven't—haven't done anything.

Not yet...

"But where did the knife come from?" My mother asks the question for what feels like the hundredth time. "And there's blood. It can't have come from nowhere, Rosanna. Just tell me."

"I—I didn't... I haven't." I pull a hand through my hair, but my hair's sticky. My hand comes away red. More blood there too—what? I look down at the floor. The knife is still there. "Mum, I haven't done anything. I woke up and...and they were at my window—they were..."

"Who?"

"The girls from my dreams, my visions...the ghosts. Mum, they look like me. They all do—all of them...a bit.

And…and there are loads. And they… I told you about her—them—before."

You're all cursed. All the Larnes and the Nobles and the Maplevens. And the curse will start over, and you will die.

My mother frowns, but I speak before she can.

"They're getting worse, Mum. I'm seeing her, seeing them everywhere. When I'm awake and…and we're all cursed." I wince as pain breaks out across my head. "All the Larnes and the Nobles and the Maplevens. And the curse will start over, and I will die."

I keep the drawing of the girl next to my pillow—the drawing the Dark Witch gave me. I don't know why. I just do. I stare at her face in the candlelight before I go to sleep each night, and there's something about her—how she's staring back—that reassures me. That makes me feel better. A connection. There's something. And it sounds mad.

But every night that I look at her face before I go to sleep, I don't have the dreams. They've gone. And that's why the Dark Witch gave me the drawing! She knew it would free me!

But she said she'd look into your visions after the first deal had been fulfilled. Not during.

I push that thought away. It's not important. All that matters is that I'm free. Free like a feather floating in the wind. Like an autumn leaf gliding down a stream.

I'm not going mad. And I'm not cursed. I can't be.

I still hear the evil fairy's voice though. But that's to be expected, I know that. Looking at the Dark Witch's photo of the girl isn't going to stop that. Agatha Tapleman agreed on that point, when I updated her—was it yesterday I saw her? Or today? I can't remember. How much time has passed since I found the knife, since my mother disposed of it? I don't know.

But I feel better now. So much better. I even heard my mother telling Elyne Taylor that I was back to normal, when she came around to help with some last-minute changes for the Dark Witch's dresses. And had Elyne treated me with just a little bit more warmth? I frown, can't remember. But it doesn't really matter what she thinks, does it? It doesn't matter what anyone thinks.

I think you're ready now.

I flinch at the fairy's voice, and then rapid anger floods me, like a stormy tide pulling in. Too much water, too much danger. What does *she* know about me? How does she know I'm ready for—

Ready for what?

More pain snakes across my forehead, and I wince, but I'm used to it now, aren't I? The pain. Her pain.

She's in me.

I'm part of her, she's part of me.

But it doesn't feel that bad, does it? Not really… Can you feel the power, Rosanna? It's growing—it's getting stronger. My power. *Your* power. We're the same.

And it doesn't feel bad anymore—because suddenly it changes. I change. The world changes. One of us does. Or both of us have.

I don't know.

And it's different. It's so different. And I don't know what's happening because it's all going too quickly, and I can't keep up—not really. But it doesn't matter, and she tells me that all the time.

Be calm.

I smile. I am calm.

The clock downstairs chimes twelve. Midnight.

My seventeenth birthday has started.

Now it is time. Let me show you.

My eyelids suddenly grow heavy. I fall asleep.

NINE

I *watch the prince as he rides through the forest of thorns on a horse as black as midnight. His hair is red—the only colour in these woods—and he wears a silver breastplate that mirrors the sharp points of the brambles. Every now and then, when he gets to a part of the path where the brambles have grown more vigorously, he dismounts from his horse and draws out a long sword. The brambles fall away, and he leads his horse through.*

Now, he stops for a rest.

From behind a tall tree, I shift my weight slightly as I watch him. I just have to kill him. If I kill him, Briar Rose will not wake. I can correct the damage that the interfering thirteenth fairy did. He cannot kiss her if he is dead. And he's the only prince who can wake her.

And then the brambles will grow and grow. An

impenetrable barrier. She will sleep and keep sleeping.

But the prince is cutting through them.

I look down at the pocket of my dress, and my hand retrieves the vial of poison. The Dark Witch is a great teacher, and now I am a great assassin.

Each day, I have killed someone. Spilled their blood, given my mother more power. Killing fills me, and now—just holding the vial of poison—I feel the adrenaline. The light catches the vial, and I see myself reflected in it—see my beautiful dark wings. I smile.

The prince mounts his horse again and rides on.

I follow, light and fast on my feet, then light and fast on the wind, my wings strong. I land on the pathway again as the prince nears the edge of the forest. He is sweating now, and his face is ruddy, red. He smears some dirt across his forehead when he wipes the back of his hand there.

Then he turns his horse, looks at me.

Looks through me.

My invisibility is strong. A smile graces my lips.

"Hello?" The prince looks worried, weak. He raises his sword, cautiously, turns his head from left to right.

I resist the urge to snort. A weak prince. Whatever would the girls in the village say?

When the prince is satisfied there is no one else

here—and has looked directly at me five more times—he gives the horse a small squeeze with his heels.

I wait until they've walked a little way before I follow.

The brambles are the thickest here. And, after a moment, the prince dismounts once more and ties his horse to an old stump. He inspects his sword, then continues walking.

I reach the horse, stroke her nose. She watches me warily. Animals either love us or hate us. I reach up and scratch her behind the ears, but she pulls her head away. I leave her and follow the prince.

Darkness pulls at the edge of the foliage. Mud seeps over my boots. Something touches my arm, and I turn, breathing hard. A lone leaf, floating carelessly. I frown and continue.

The path turns to the left ahead, and the prince has disappeared from sight. My heart pounds with adrenaline— with anticipation—and I speed up. My fingers start to sweat; I grip the vial of poison tighter.

I round the corner. My eyes narrow.

He is not here.

The prince is not here.

Something snaps behind me.

I freeze, then turn—turn and—

A flash of broken sunlight on metal.

A sharp intake of breath.

A glimpse of red and—

And then there's only darkness.

I wake up on a cold floor, my face pressed against the marble, like my frozen soul. Pain ensnares every sinew of my body and the moment I lift my head I feel the wounds on my back. My breath comes in heavy bursts as I force myself to sit up, as I twist my head, as I see.

My wings, broken, bruised. Feathers hacked off. And burning—the smell of burnt feathers and smoke clings to me. Bile rises in my throat, and I steel myself, try to move my wings, try to—

Pain unfolds and I cry out. My vision darkens and the world tips.

I fall, hit my head. Darkness and white lights, and when I open my eyes, I see metal bars that stretch on and on, falling into the abyss only to be spat out. Forced back into the world of the living and—

Footsteps.

I freeze, my heart pounding.

He's getting closer.

He's coming.

The prince—the prince who broke my wings—is coming for me.

Every part of me screams for me to get up, for me to fight him, to make him hurt like I'm hurting, but I can't. My head's too heavy, and I can't...can't think now... There's only pain. So much pain. Torrents of it, and the room's filling with it. Pain that submerges my wings, disintegrates each individual feather.

Step.

Step.

Step.

And then he's here, his face pressed against the metal bars.

I manage to lift my head, try to snarl at him.

The prince looks at me. His eyes brim with disgust and anger, and he takes a box of matches from his pocket.

"Tell me your name."

I shake my head, and the movement pulls at the wounds on my back. Tears pierce the corners of my eyes.

The prince strikes the match slowly; a bead of fire is born.

"It would be a pity if your wings were burnt completely off this time, wouldn't it?"

TEN

I wake, gasping, spluttering, out of breath, drenched in sweat. I sit up, the covers are tight around me, and for a moment I fight them, convinced they are hands.

Do you see now? I am trapped, tortured. Still! But you can rescue me. You must rescue me, Rosanna—you are the only one I can show the way to. Rescue me, and I will stop the ogress from getting you.

I inhale so hard it hurts my lungs. The ogress? My visions—my visions of the girls being *murdered* by ogresses and—

My chest squeezes and I look up—and for a second, I think I see an ogress, outside the window. My scream catches in my throat, and I feel cold fingers on me. I turn, breathing hard, and—

It's the curse, the fairy says. **It's hereditary. Those girls—the visions you've seen. They were your ancestors. And with every repetition of the curse a new girl with Larne blood is selected and she will die on her seventeenth birthday at the hands of the ogress.**

Seventeenth birthday.

My heart pounds. It's my seventeenth birthday today.

And you're next, Rosanna.

The fairy hiccups, and suddenly I feel the pain she is in—it pours into me as if thrown down a channel, gushing into me—and I gasp. There's…there's so much.

Tonight—you shall die tonight as the curse repeats, she says. **But if you save me, if you free me, I can stop it. I have enough power at the moment because *your* power is peaking and we are one soul, and I now have the strength to tell you all, to speak freely, to make you understand, to resist my captor! But, Rosanna, you must save me *now*. Your power's at its summit now; the more you delay, the less power we will both have when you find me. And the less power I have, the less likely it is that I can save you and destroy the curse. Find me now and you won't die.**

My breathing quickens.

I wait for her voice, for her next words, but she doesn't speak any more.

I look up and—a girl, in front of me.

My body jolts. The ghost. One of the ghosts. She's back.

The ogress murdered me, the girl whispers. *It's real. My seventeenth birthday. Don't let her get you too. Don't let the curse repeat. The fairy tried to help me, but I wasn't quick enough. But you can be.*

My mouth dries. I try to speak, but then she's gone and—

Darkness. So dark. A pool of blackness around me.

I reach for the candle, light it, breathing hard and—

Someone else is in the room.

I see their shadow, hear their breathing.

My pulse quickens. I reach for the heavy book by my bed, grip it hard, and—

The person steps out from the shadows, out to the foot of my bed and—

"Felix?" I peer at him. My knuckles click, I'm still gripping the book.

He stares at me.

"Come on, Rosanna," he whispers. "We have to go."

My heart pounds. My fingers cling to the book, as if they've got a life of their own, and gripping onto the tome is their sole purpose.

Felix holds his hand out to me.

"What?"

"We're running away! You're seventeen—Happy Birthday!—but we can get married now. We can do it now, just go and—"

I get out of bed slowly, stand up. Something inside me clicks. "Marriage?"

"If we're married, they can't officially engage me to Carolina," Felix says, and my head whirls faster and faster. "We'll be together. But we have to go now, I've found a priest who'll marry us, even given your condition, but we can't keep him waiting. Come on, you agreed to this."

I stare at him. "What? This—I didn't—"

"We talked about it yesterday. Before you set off to the Dark Witch's castle to deliver the dresses."

I shake my head. "That... I didn't...there were no dresses to do yesterday."

That's right, isn't it? No. I frown. But my hands start to tremble. I can't remember. Why can't I remember? But everything's a blur, and there are just images, little flashes of things.

"There *were*," Felix says, and he says it in such a way that I instantly want to believe him. A part of me does. Because he's my friend, my only friend, and I should believe him because he's always been there for me. "You can't have forgotten… Rosanna?"

He's trying to distract you, make you doubt yourself! Come and save me and I shall save you.

Blackness fills my mind, it's like tar. So sticky and gloopy, spreading itself farther and farther, covering every thought.

"Rosanna?" Felix's face wobbles, but I'm looking at him through the tar—through a thin layer that stretches and stretches until it breaks and I see him clearly. "Are you okay?"

"Yes," I say.

Then I look across at the drawing of the girl, the one the Dark Witch gave me. My ancestor?

And she died because of a curse—a curse that's going to get me?

The cycle must stop, daughter. A circle can end. It must.

Help me, and I will help you.

Come, join me.

Save me.

I've been waiting for you for ages—for the girl who can break the curse.

Several moments pass. I wait for more of her words,

but none come.

I stand up, look out the window. It's dark and hazy out there, but I can see it's still snowing.

"Okay," I whisper.

ELEVEN

"Where are you going?" Felix's shout stops me in my tracks, and the wind howls around me.

I turn back, look at him.

"We have to go this way." He gestures behind him. "The priest is waiting at the Newberry Inn." He takes a small step towards me.

My heart pounds, my head pounds, everything pounds.

I look around, see the wolves. They're hiding in the foliage. Felix hasn't noticed them.

And amongst them is a winged creature—a creature I've never seen before.

A sour tang spreads across the back of my tongue as I stare at it. It's small, whatever it is. About three feet high. And stocky, thickly-set limbs. Its head is turned away from me, and long dark hair drips down the centre of its back. Either side of the trail of hair, two wide gnashes have been burnt into its skin, and it's from the middle of these gnashes that tattered black feathers protrude.

My bottom lip curls and I cover my mouth.

And then it flickers. The whole thing flickers, and for a moment I see the fur of the wolf that stands behind the creature. See the wolf as if the creature's not there at all.

"Is that you?" I ask, my words breathy and light.

Follow me. I cannot project for long.

"Of course it's me," Felix shouts.

I turn back, see him several feet away. He lifts his arms in the air. "What are you doing? Come on, it's this way."

No, this way. We haven't got long.

"Uh, yes," I say, looking at Felix. "I—I need to get my dress."

He frowns. "So you *did* get one?"

"I made it," I lie. "I'm the Dark Witch's dressmaker, Felix... It's in the coal shed...but we need something else..."

"What?" He looks blank.

My head spins. The ogress... If she comes for me today... Oh, God. I need to be prepared. "Poison," I say, and it seems right. And I *know* it's right. "I need poison."

"Poison?" Felix stares at me.

And then his eyes seem to get too big—and I can see them so clearly—and those blue pools are too big. I see myself floating in them. Floating head down on the water.

"Are you…?" Felix swears under his breath, then takes a step backwards. "Rosanna, you…you need to… I think the evil fairy is…is controlling you…"

Pain inches into me.

I dip a splinter of flax in the dark purple liquid, hold it up in the sunlight, watch as the potion dries clear on the wood.

I blink hard. Dizziness takes hold of me and I stumble backward, don't know where that image came from.

Get the poison!

I turn, and I run. Run towards the wolves, over to where they're hiding; it's the winged wight I need.

Don't worry, they won't see you—the wolves won't see you, I'll make sure of it.

Felix calls after me, but he doesn't follow.

The ghostly winged creature leads me to the Dark Witch's castle, and when I get there, she's holding a vial. A vial of dark purple liquid.

I take it from her, breathless, tuck the vial into my belt.

"Be quick, daughter. It must happen tonight. If not, you will never be free, and I will always be alone."

Her words tumble over me. But I haven't got time to think. Can't think.

I run, run after the winged wight as she flits away from me. She's weakening already—I can barely see her. And then—and then she's gone, but she still speaks into my mind, tells me where to go.

And anger fuels me. I see images of the cages she's been kept in, and I feel the pain as her wings are burnt off, over and over again.

My mouth sets into a firm line.

The prince with the red hair, he has the fairy somewhere. My fairy. Imprisoned. And I've got to find her.

This way. Hurry!

And I do hurry. The world hurries.

I run for hours and hours—hours that feel like days. And I feel my body getting weaker, but I can't stop, can't think about roast chicken and beef brisket and bacon and duck. Food's not important. I don't need food. Food is a distraction—and the people who spring up before me with plates of roast chicken and steaming vegetables are evil spirits designed to stop me. They want the fairy to be imprisoned forever.

But she has to be free.

I am her.

Our souls are the same.

We're the same.

And you'll kill for me, and I'll kill for you.

And I nod and agree, and at some point—I don't know how long I've been travelling—I see the winged wight again—see her, and—

Someone screams.

Ice dives into my veins, and I turn, see an old woman and a boy.

The old woman points at me, and her finger shakes. "Stay away! And take your curses with you! Don't bring death to my door!"

I shrink away from her.

Keep running!

My feet slam the snow into compacted footprints, and I run so fast I feel like I must be flying. The world blurs past me, and I sprint through woods, through villages, around lakes, over bridges.

And I run so fast that I can barely keep up; it feels like my mind could get left behind.

This way, the fairy tells me. **You're close. So close.**

And her voice is louder now, so much louder. I feel her voice in me, can detect the tension in her tone, her emotions. Excitement? Apprehension?

I look up; a city is in the distance. No snow. But the air's hazy and blue, laced with cold. Am I still in the Snow Kingdom? Or crossing over to a new region?

Come faster—I'm losing my power!

And then I'm in the city. So quickly. Moving without realising it, and everything's a blur, going too fast. Time's going too fast.

Buildings rush around me—great, huge buildings made from huge slabs of stone—and a clock tower strikes the hour. I try to count the bells, but I can't because I feel so sick and my head's giddy.

I force myself to stop, even though my legs protest. My head pounds and I look to my left. There's a fountain of water a few feet away, and I walk over to it, cup my hands and dip them into the water. It's cold, but there's a softness to it too. Like silk. Delicate.

I sip the water and—

I see her face reflected from the pool's rippling surface—the face of one of the murdered girls. Her eyes are wide, frozen, and she stares at me. And then—then cracks appear in her face, across her skin, getting deeper and deeper.

I watch her disintegrate. Until she's gone.

Hurry! Otherwise, that will be you too!

I run as fast as I can again—always running, just running—until my lungs are screaming and my legs are aching and sweat is dripping from me. But I have to keep going.

And you will! Quickly! Almost there.

I turn down a side street, my bare feet smacking the cobbled stones. Part of me knows that running down here should be painful on my feet, but I feel nothing. The smell of smoked kippers wraps around me, clings to me, and I breathe deeply.

Food…food…food…

My eyes start to water, and my mouth feels strange. My tongue aches.

No! Keep going! Go through the city! We're almost there!

My feet take me through a dark alleyway, and a drunk man leers at me. But power races through my veins, and then I'm out of there, running faster than I ever thought was possible, so fast that my feet barely seem to touch the ground.

The stone cobbles turn into wet grass, and then the land tips into a valley. Thick green vines grow overhead, make a mesh that I weave expertly through as if I've been here before and know the exact layout.

The air is strangely humid, warm, and alive for this time of year. Insects buzz. The ground is damp, and I look down, see my feet disappearing into the squelchy grassland.

Ahead, a lone stone house rises out of the woodland floor at a strange angle, as if the marsh is trying to claim it. I frown as I look at the building. The architecture is more like that of a castle than a home. Though it's nothing compared to the Dark Witch's abode.

Go!

I reach it in seconds, splashing through waterlogged grass.

There! That window!

I look up, feel jolted, jarred, as if the fairy's commanding my head and not me. I stare at the building, the great slabs of grey stone and the moss and ivy that climb up high. One window pokes out at the top, three storeys high. The glass looks old, and an elm's twig fingers dance against it, scratching.

I'm in there! Let me out!

I race around the side of the building, see a door, and I

run towards it, grab the handle.

Be quick! My powers are seeping away... You're taking too long!

"I'm here!" I yell.

I turn the handle, push open the door, and—

Something hits me hard across the face. I stagger back, twist to the side, and something bangs behind me—the door? I turn, but it's dark, can't see anything, can't—

Hands land on my arms.

But they're not hands. Not human.

They're claws. Cold and strangely slimy.

My stomach hardens.

No.

No.

No.

I look up and what little bit of light there is in this room suddenly illuminates her face.

"Excellent, you came just in time," my aunt says. "I *am* hungry."

TWELVE

I stare at my aunt. My pulse quickens and I blink rapidly, but she doesn't change. It's her—really her. Aunt Keres.

Kill her! Kill her with the poison!

But I don't move my hand towards my belt where the vial is tucked in. My hands stay frozen by my sides, and my legs tighten painfully.

"Shall we start dinner?" My aunt smiles, and then she guides me into the room, her hand on my shoulder.

I turn my head, try to see that hand…and it is just a hand. A normal human hand. No claws. I was wrong… I panicked earlier, and my imagination got the better of me. I gulp and look around. The room is dark and bare and—

Movement catches my eyes and my gaze jerks up. They're all around the room, the dead girls, haunting me. And the more I look, the more of them I see. Five, six, seven, eight… All girls like me. The same eyes and—

So many of them.

Each with a tear-drop scar. And I see the marks everywhere—the marks of the fairy's possessions. On hands, on faces, on shoulders, on necks.

We're all cursed, one of them whispers, and her voice is pure. *Cursed because of our blood.*

"Sit down," my aunt says, and she smiles widely.

I look around for the chairs, but there aren't any. There's nothing. Nothing in here except for my aunt, myself, and the dead girls.

Kill her! And set me free! Kill—

My aunt lunges for me, and I don't see her hand in time. Just feel the sting of the slap as I fall down. And then she pounces, and her weight's on me, pushing me onto the floorboards. I scream, and I cry out, try to kick and—

Her face hovers above me.

And slowly, so slowly, her skin starts to peel. It peels away, like the bark of a silver birch. Flakes of it drop off, land on the wooden floor. My stomach twists, and my throat suddenly feels too thick, as if it's swelling up.

Underneath her peeling skin, my aunt's face has a green tinge. Her teeth elongate, and a string of saliva drips from her mouth.

Rosanna!

My breathing quickens. The string of saliva breaks and lands on my face.

Don't be like the others! They were too slow! They were killed before they had a chance to move! But you're strong, Rosanna. Think and act! Kill her to save us both, and you'll be rewarded.

My aunt shakes herself, and the rest of her human skin falls off, onto me, and—

I jump to my feet, but the ogress is too big—she towers over me and—

How can she be so big?

My *aunt*?

My heart pounds. She tries to grab me, and I let out a scream, throw myself to the side. My feet skid on the floorboards, splinters in my feet and—

One of the murdered girls throws something towards me, and it clatters on the floor.

I look down—a knife.

The knife—the same one as before. I pick it up, and it is…it's the murder weapon. The one that killed this girl, the weapon the ogress used.

I grab it, turn—

The ogress screams as I swipe the knife across her

arm, slash it and—

Silver blood pours out. For a second, I freeze, fascinated.

Kill her! Use the poison!

The fairy's voice jars me, and I flinch, look around and—

A flash of green, and then claws swipe across my face. I shriek, fall backwards, clutch the knife to me as I try to get up, but there's silver blood here too, and it's slippery. I reach out, a hand against the clammy wall.

The ogress advances, and her eyes bulge like overripe apples.

"Stay back! Or I'll hurt you again!" I yell, gripping the knife as hard as I can, but my fingers are sweaty, and my grip keeps slackening, and the whole time the fairy yells at me to use the poison. "I mean it!"

But the ogress doesn't stay back. She keeps coming forward, closer, closer, closer.

"You wouldn't want to hurt your mother, would you?" the ogress whispers, but her voice sounds more like Aunt Keres's now, and it makes my chest feel strange.

I go cold. "My mother?" I look around, expect to see her. "Where is she? What have you done to her?"

"Me? Oh, I haven't done anything. But, then again,

Louisa Mapleven is *not* your biological mother."

My muscles tense in my throat, a quick bout of pain there, sharp.

"You want to know who is?" The ogress reaches me, and there's something about her eyeballs—how they're swelling as she stares at me—that makes my stomach twist.

Kill her!

I try to move the knife, but I can't. My fingers, they won't work. Nothing will. My mother—not my mother? Rushing sounds fill my ears, and my heart pounds.

"Do you want to know, my sweet little warrior?" The ogress leans in closer and—

Kill her! You're losing power and—

The ogress laughs. "*Me*. You are mine, made *just* for me. A princess of two long-forgotten royal lines. The perfect meal."

My blood turns to ice.

I stare at her.

My breaths make a scratching noise against my throat.

No.

No.

No.

I shake my head, reach for the vial of poison tucked in my belt. "Stop it! You're not—"

"I am! Oh, Rosanna, I have been looking forward to you for so long. Those fleeting visits—the glimpse of you each year—just made my appetite sweeter." A gong sounds somewhere in the distance, and the ogress licks her lips. "Dinner time!"

She grabs me, claws jabbing my skin, and—

A flash of her teeth and—

"No!" I scream, and somehow in one quick motion, the glass vial in my hand smashes, the purple liquid drenches the blade, and I plunge the knife into the ogress's chest, into her heart.

Her body shudders and her eyes latch onto mine—my aunt's face, her human form appearing as she tries to change, and I stare at her eyes and…and… *my* eyes. They're my eyes too. Brown. Dark, but bulging and—

I've always had big eyes.

My body locks up. And then she falls. Crashes to the ground. Still. So still.

And she's dead. I know she's dead. I feel it, actually *feel* it.

My *mother*?

Something hardens in my chest.

My head pounds, and there's too much stuff racing around inside it. And—

Metal breaks. Snaps like thin twigs. Click. Click. Click.

I am free!

I jump, hear footsteps behind me. I turn slowly, my heart pounding, pounding, pounding.

I see her.

A small woman, with wizened skin. Long fingernails that twist together in a writhing mass descend down each side. Her hair is black and straight, but thin. So thin. Like spun sugar. And it's moving now, each strand lifting up.

For a second, her image flickers, and for the smallest of times, her wings are visible. Broken, battered, beyond repair, and—

But the wight looks different. Not like the last time I saw her. She's changing, growing stronger and more beautiful, like the first time I saw her, when the sky turned red. When she chose me.

I am free now, thank you.

I look at her, point slowly at her, then at the body of the ogress behind me. I open my mouth, feel my lips buzz as I try to form words. But I can't. I stare at the fairy, at the ogress, at the room around me as everything spins and pounds.

The fairy smiles and steps closer. How can she be

smiling? It doesn't…

She lifts her hands to my face, and, as her cold fingers touch me, I gasp. Her eyes brighten a little, and she blinks slowly. Dust falls from her long lashes.

Thank you. You're one of us now. But let me show you, let me start at the beginning.

And suddenly I feel her in my mind again; I feel her fingers placing images there for me to see. Images that move.

A tiny baby, a christening. Watching from the back of the room. Fairies go up, one by one, and give their gifts… Waiting, waiting, waiting.

A nudge against my side. The Dark Witch. "They've forgotten you—left you out."

Anger. So much anger, and it's building, building, building. A volcano of anger and magma rises. Pressure builds.

I part the crowd with a flick of my fingers, and my wings burn with fury. The king and queen look up at me with horror in their eyes.

I point at the baby, darling Briar Rose Larne, heiress to the Thorn Kingdom. "She shall prick her finger on a spinning wheel and die!"

Hushed voices, and I'm pushed away.

Another fairy. "Not death, but one hundred years of soft sleep from which a prince shall wake her."

"Destroy all spinning wheels."

"Kill all the princes," the Dark Witch whispers to me. "If no princes live when the time for Briar Rose's awakening comes, she will die. Your curse—the original curse—will take over if more than a hundred years have passed."

"How dare you try to kill my son!" the ogress screams and then she says my name because of course she knows it, and the shackles bind me to her for life. "But you didn't succeed, did you? And he will wake the princess, and she will bear his children and I will drink the blood of my first granddaughter and eat her flesh."

From my window, I watch the cook serve up Briar Rose's girl. I watch the ogress pick up her knife and fork, and I watch as she slices the flesh. I hear the smack of her lips as she chews. The way her eyes move back and forth.

"This ain't the Larne girl!"

And she looks up at me for a second, and then the cook runs out of the castle, to the outside table where the ogress sits. He's out of breath, and his face is red.

"You thought you could fool me? I need Larne blood! It is the sweetest, even more so when it is mixed with my own in a granddaughter."

"A granddaughter?" The prince appears from behind a tree, fury in his eyes. Briar Rose's other child—the boy—is with him, and the prince pushes the toddler behind him. "You tried to eat my daughter?"

He takes a knife from the inside of his jacket.

The image disappears and then I'm back in the room—the room with the fairy and the ogress's body. I start to turn to look at her, then stop. I can't look at her.

When the prince killed his mother—the ogress—the curse I set on Briar Rose repeated, the fairy says. **And when the ogress awoke one hundred years later, she was starving. She wanted Larne blood—wanted it like she's never wanted anything before. Being tricked by the cook had only made her desire stronger, and she vowed that she'd only feed on the female Larne descendants of her granddaughter from now on. Nothing would stop her.**

She looks away suddenly, her gaze dropping to the floor.

A fairy's name is powerful, and she knew my name

because her son told her. Her shoulders droop, and she trembles. **I have been trapped here by her, aiding her plans, for centuries... She cannot often leave her swamp, her small kingdom—her job at the Royal Castle of the Snow Kingdom was a cover-up.**

And she needed me. It is difficult for a full ogress to maintain a human image, and, during her hundred-year sleep, the branch of the Larne bloodline she was interested in had moved from the Thorn Kingdom to lands far away, spreading farther with each new generation as marriages were made, as kingdoms came together and others dissolved...until the girls' royalty was forgotten and buried. My mistress couldn't make the journeys to the Larne girls often, and so she needed me to do most of the contact with the selected girls, to *ensure* they still came to her on the evening when their blood was best. And every hundred years, the ogress needed new Larne blood, and she wanted it sweetened by her ogre lineage—just as it would've been with her first granddaughter—but with every hundred years that passed, the ogre lineage in the chosen Larne bloodline reduced dramatically, until there was none. And so, she began posing as a human on the nights she was strongest and marrying into the family, trying to produce a half-

ogress daughter whom she could feed from and satisfy her cravings.

My stomach twists, and then one of the dead girls meets my eyes. We both shudder.

But, for centuries, the ogress bore only sons, and sons were no good to her. Their blood is bitter. She still had to rely on daughters the Larne women produced— for she *had* to eat—but she was forced to forego the powerful ogre lineage in their blood. She made me lure the girls to her on the evenings of their seventeenth birthdays—the time when Larne blood is the strongest. And, each time, on those nights, I became more powerful too, and I tried to get the girls to act, to kill the ogress and stop the curse. But every time, the Larne girls failed.

I flinch. The ghosts of the girls close in. They're all listening. I look past them, stare at the off-white walls. Damp is creeping up from the floor, and I sniff the air, notice for the first time how musty it is in here. I don't know why that seems important, but it does.

The fairy clears her throat. **The curse kept repeating, but then *you* were born.** Now she lifts her head and looks at me with her full gaze. **You were born to the ogress, Rosanna. The perfect meal—a girl-child with Larne blood and ogre lineage was what she desired most of all.**

What she lived to taste.

I shake my head. "But I'm *not* related to her. She's my aunt—I'm no blood relation at all."

But the fairy shakes her head. **The ogress was your mother, posing as a human. What she said was true.**

My heart thumps, and I shake my head more vigorously. "No. My mother is—"

She swapped you! The ogress swapped you. You and your cousin were born on the same day—she had me use my magic to ensure the dates would be the same. And your mother swapped you. She didn't want to become close, knowing she would eat you. She wanted to be distant.

I snort, think about what Carolina said. She was distant with her too. Playing 'mother' to her didn't make any difference. Not really.

She raised Louisa's child as her own, gave Carolina her full love. She told me your name, Rosanna. Made me lure you in. I was in your head—sometimes I separated from your body, watched you for a moment or two—*I* chose to lead you to the Dark Witch to get the poison. But I *had* to bring you here, to her—the ogress. I had no choice—she controlled me. What she didn't know was that you would be spilling the blood, not her, as you

broke the curse.

I feel sick, strange, dizzy. I stare at the fairy, feel sick. I look down at my body. Ogre lineage?

Then I look at the ogress. Look at her properly. At least seven feet tall, sprawled out ungracefully, a snarl trapped forever on her face—her face that holds its human façade.

"Rosanna!"

The shout makes me jump, and I turn. *Felix*? His voice—that was…

The door opens suddenly, and he marches in. Behind him are my mother, Carolina, and my uncle. Or—or my father? My head pounds.

I look back to the fairy, but she's gone. Disappeared. Invisible. The girls have gone too. All I see are the murky damp patches on the walls.

It's just me. Me and them, and my aunt's body. The ogress's body.

"We came after you!" Felix cries. "I realised the evil fairy was possessing you, and I got help! Your mother, your uncle, and Carolina! They said your aunt's at the Royal Castle working, so she couldn't come, but—" His words fall away.

Carolina makes a choking noise and my gaze jolts to

her. She stares at me, at the knife in my hand by my side. I'd forgotten I was holding it. Her eyes go to her mother's body. No, *my* mother's body and—

"Your aunt's here?" Felix says, and he stares at her. "Why isn't she at the Royal Castle? That's *miles and miles* away and—"

"What have you done?" My mother's voice shakes, and she looks up at me and—

"Rosanna?" Felix's eyes widen, and I don't understand why they're not asking why Aunt Keres has an ogress's body.

Carolina screams and throws herself at me, and—

And I lift my arms, try to stop her from crashing into me, from knocking us both down.

Try to—

The poisoned knife slices into her flesh.

Her beautiful eyes look at me. The same as my mother's…the woman who raised me.

My mother—but hers too.

Carolina screams.

I let go of the knife. The handle sticks out of her chest. Carolina looks down at it. Her face pales.

Deathly pale.

She falls. Graceful, unlike the ogress. And that seems

important. I don't know why, but it does. My teeth chatter as I stare at her. I feel something twist in my gut, and a heavy sense of darkness spreads across my body. My heart speeds up until it's racing, racing so fast and—

"Carolina?" My voice is a whisper.

I swallow hard. My stomach twists and then there are sharp pains running through my body, radiating from my shoulder blades. I'm shaking.

"Carolina!"

But I don't move, not towards her. I can't move.

Felix and my mother look on. My uncle lets out a strangled cry as if he's only just realised what's happened—what I've done. And we're—we're all standing still. Statues. And then my mother breaks the stillness and wheels her chair towards me. It squeaks. She stops three feet from me. There is fire in her eyes, and it burns me.

Run, one of the murdered girl's shouts. *You've broken the Curse of the Winged Wight—no more girls will die at the hand of the ogress—but for goodness sake, run!*

THIRTEEN

Once upon a time, there was a cottage where ivy and roses grew up the walls, on trellises made of the finest willow.

The girl who lived in the cottage was beautiful. The most beautiful in all the land. Clear skin, like fresh snow, with just the right amount of blush dancing across her face. Dark eyes—big, wide, stunning. Crimson lips that one thought had to be painted on because they were so perfect. And her hair! Sleek blond locks that spilled across her shoulders, tumbling down her torso in baby ringlets.

We all know the type of girl I'm talking about. The type who is a princess—she just is. It doesn't matter that she's not the daughter of the king and queen, or that she doesn't live in a castle.

She's still the girl that every little girl wants to be.

And really, she was perfect.

So perfect, and I killed her.

I didn't mean to.

Now you're like me, the fairy whispers as we travel the countryside. **Despised by all. Never to be trusted again. A black mark hangs over us. I started it all, the curse that killed your ancestors. I tried to kill Briar Rose, a beautiful girl. I failed. I started all this—but you have ended it. You succeeded in destroying the ogress, destroying the curse.**

It's snowing and the air is bitter.

And you killed a beautiful girl. Did what I could not. She smiles. **At last, one of you managed it.**

She smiles widely at me.

My bottom lip wobbles. I think of the way my mother looked at me earlier. "What am I going to do? Where am I to go?"

My mother, the fairy says. **Yessssss, we will go to my mother. She has been keeping you safe, keeping you close, ever since I connected with you. That made us family, and she didn't want to lose any more grandchildren. And you were her latest hope to save me, Rosanna, for she couldn't find me and I couldn't possess**

her to tell her, even if the ogress had allowed me to.

And now you shall live with us, for as long as we live—a great gift, Rosanna. No other humans with ogre lineage have lived longer than their human lives…but you shall, because it is my gift to you, my thank you.

Come on, you know the way to my mother's castle. We shall go there, *daughter*.

The Dark Witch greets us warmly. Her smile makes me uneasy. She shows me to a small room where there is a large mirror, and I stare at it. I see black feathers framing my back. I frown, and turn, look over my shoulder—look at nothing, because there's nothing there…but the mirror?

I blink rapidly as I stare at my reflection again.

Behind me, the Dark Witch lets out a small laugh. I look up, see her behind me. And—and she's got them too. Wings…just like the fairy's.

We're *both* like her.

I turn, dazed, and the Dark Witch smiles, starts talking. She says this room is to be mine and I am to call her *Grandmother*.

She says she has a job for me.

She gives me a bow and arrow and a necklace made of silver and angels' tears.

"The wolves' numbers are getting too big. Protect the villagers. My daughter will keep you safe."

AUTHOR'S NOTE:
RETELLING THE FAIRY TALE

"The Curse of the Winged Wight" is my first fairy tale retelling; writing it was a very different process to my other (dystopian) works, and so it was both refreshing and a challenge. From the start, I knew I wanted my fairy tale retelling to be inspired by the Sleeping Beauty fairy tale, and upon researching the origin of this tale, I was astounded by just how many versions there were, and how the details and plot changed with each retelling, due to the oral tradition of the genre.

After much reading, I discovered that it was Charles Perrault's "The Sleeping Beauty" (first published in 1697) that inspired me the most. In particular it was the darkness prevalent in Perrault's tale that really gripped me—as well as the ogress—and so I went on to read the tale that Perrault's story was based on: "Sun, Moon, and Talia" by Giambattista Basile (published in 1634). I also turned to "Briar Rose" and "The In-Law-Mother" by the Brothers Grimm, (both published in the 1812 collection), two fairy tales that, when put together, very closely resemble

Perrault's "The Sleeping Beauty", to see how much Perrault's story had changed due to the oral transmission of fairy tales, in just over a hundred years. Reading these three versions of the same story not only inspired me greatly, but it also gave me a strong understanding of how a single fairy tale evolves over time as it is retold, giving me a good background of the origins of the Sleeping Beauty fairy tale.

It was at this stage that I felt ready to begin my own retelling, where I would weave something new into the story to take it in a different direction and give it a different emphasis to its previous versions. The old fairy in Perrault's tale was my starting place as whenever I've heard the Sleeping beauty tale I've wanted to know more about her. Yet, at the same time, I also wanted to have a sense of mystery about the fairy. Sure, she was important, but I wanted my readers to see her through another's eyes and never quite be sure of who this fairy was and what she was really like. And, thus, my main character, Rosanna Mapleven, was born and I immediately knew that she'd be possessed by the fairy. The more I wrote of Rosanna, the more I came to love her as a narrator due to the complexities of her character, the love triangle she's wrapped up in, and her relationship to the evil fairy.

I've always loved gothic fiction, and as I was writing

an early draft of "The Curse of the Winged Wight", I realised I wanted my retelling to have a gothic feel to it too, and so I decided to introduce a hereditary curse and ghostly apparitions to my loose retelling of the Sleeping Beauty fairy tale. And from that decision onwards, the story blossomed and the characters led the plot. I couldn't write fast enough as I drew on aspects of my chosen source material by Perrault, Basile, and the Brothers Grimm, and fused these with my own imagination and characters, as well as my love for stories about entrapment and injustice, family and inheritance, wolves and fairies.

I hope you've enjoyed reading "The Curse of the Winged Wight" just as much as I enjoyed writing it.

ACKNOWLEDGEMENTS

Writing my first fairy tale retelling has been so much fun.

I'd like to acknowledge Charles Perrault's "The Sleeping Beauty" (1697), "Sun, Moon, and Talia" by Giambattista Basile (published in 1634), and "Briar Rose" and "The In-Law-Mother", two tales collected and recorded by the Brothers Grimm in 1812, as these stories were instrumental in my research into the origins of the Sleeping Beauty tale as well as my understanding of the literary and oral traditions of the genre. It was so much fun reading these stories, examining how the Sleeping Beauty fairy tale changed across the centuries, and using them to spark a new narrative based on this famous fairy tale.

Many thanks must go to my first readers for all their help and the many read-throughs of the countless older drafts of "The Curse of the Winged Wight": Elizabetta Holcomb, Rachael Bundy, Lizzie Colt, and Alice Rachel—thank you for your insightful comments and suggestions, and for assessing each new draft, and giving me your honest feedback. Equally, thanks must also go to Ria Hockey,

Samantha Martin, and Claire Connon for your feedback on the representation of disability within this story. It was very important to me to get this portrayal right and I value your feedback greatly. Thank you for taking the time to read and discuss it with me.

To my wonderful editor, Michelle Dunbar: you went above and beyond my expectations in your editing of this story. I'm very grateful to you, and would love to work with you again.

Mum, Dad, and Sam—thank you, as always, for believing in me and my writing. Your support means a lot.

And finally, to the rest of my family, my friends, and my readers—thank you. I hope you enjoyed this story.

ABOUT THE AUTHOR

Madeline Dyer lives on a farm in the southwest of England, where she hangs out with her Shetland ponies and writes young adult books—sometimes, at the same time. She holds a BA Honours degree in English from the University of Exeter, and several presses have published her fiction. Madeline has a strong love for anything dystopian, ghostly, or paranormal, and she can frequently be found exploring wild places. At least one notebook is known to follow her wherever she goes.

"The Curse of the Winged Wight" is her first novella.

ALSO BY MADELINE DYER

The Untamed Series

Untamed

Fragmented

Divided

Coming Soon

Destroyed

* 9 7 8 1 9 1 2 3 6 9 0 1 0 *